There's a Light

Let the Light Shine Through

Pamela J Spears

There's A Light

References from KJV bible scriptures,

Cover picture by Pamela L. Aaron

Published in the United State of America

ISBN: 979-8-45960-823-6

1.   Juvenile Fiction, Religious, Short stories

Dedication

All praises to our Lord and Savior Jesus Christ

Thank you to my family and friends for love and support.

Table of Contents

Radiance

Radiance

1

Her name was Radiance. With a name like that, you could imagine how she would shine. She would be full of joy and anticipation of greatness.

Radiance, was a happy child. Her parents felt so blessed, just to hear her chatter on and on about her imaginary friends. She always spoke of love and family and helping others. She enjoyed life. She wanted to share with every one she met. Her mom would always tell her not to bother people. She did not understand at the time but with age she would come to a better understanding.

Radiance was a sure sentiment that love shows from the inside out. Love must be in your heart to show on the outside.

An act of kindness alone is good, but when you give an act of kindness with love, it really shines and melts hearts all around.

Jesus offered the Samaritan women water from the well. She first saw water but when she realized the love, she ran to tell others.

When Peter healed Dorcas, the widow told him of all the coats and garments she had made for others. This was the love that led them to seek Peter to heal Dorcas.

There was something special about Radiance. She desired to make others smile.

Love is patient, love is kind. It does not envy, it does not boast, it is not proud. [5] It does not dishonor others, it is not self-seeking, it is not easily angered, it keeps no record of wrongs.

1 Corinthians 13: 4,5

2

One step of miss-judgment led Radiance to a life of despair, wondering how she had come to this empty space in life. Everyone was beginning to notice the change in her. It was almost as if she was no longer there.

She began to settle for things she would normally not choose. She was a bit sad or maybe gloomy is the right word. She even noticed when she looked in the mirror but there was no desire to change.   The spark somehow was gone.

She was much different as a child. She always smiled; it was like a cheerful glow. To most people this was a welcome attribute. To others it caused envy and jealousy to form in their hearts.

  This was not her fault but the results of pain in their lives. Sure, they wanted, to feel what she felt but they would never admit it.

This happens every day. We reject the joy of others because of our own pain and sorrow.

Her mom knew everyone was not willing to receive joy from anyone, child or adult.

I have heard it said laughter is contagious, but not to one who has formed a hard heart. It reminds me of the Grinch who steals Christmas. He wanted to take away the joy the Woo's felt while celebrating on Christmas Day. It is a sad thought, when one can't even find happiness within themselves.

Radiance had a way of inspiring others to do well and to believe in themselves. You can relate her to one of the disciples in the Bible. He was called an encourager.

Somewhere along the way she lost the spark she had. She no longer displayed that radiant smile everyone loved. To look upon her, sadness showed through. She walked with her head hung down, her smile was gone. The spirit of joy was no longer with her.

What happened to her was so heavy of a weight, she carried it with her every minute of the day.

There is so much in life one can encounter that would leave them void, living but with no life. What was on her mind? She would never speak the words yet, the statement, the silence made "shouted" out to all who knew

her.

For I am convinced that neither death nor life, neither angels nor demons, neither the present nor the future, nor any powers, 39 neither height nor depth, nor anything else in all creation, will be able to separate us from the love of God that is in Christ Jesus our Lord.

Roman 8:38-39

3

Radiance was doing really well but she allowed something or someone to pierce her heart. She could not have been aware of the darkness introduced to her. It was dressed as good but it was actually evil.

Where there is good evil is always present.

Radiance could always see the good in a person. This time she saw the good and ignored the evil. We always see the green grass in the meadow but not the snake on the ground.

Why do we think there is good behind every smile? Have we not heard it said, "Everyone that smiles at you is not your friend?" It would be wise to judge a smile by the sincerity of the heart, which would be shown in one's actions.

Can a person smile while committing an evil act? What kind of a person would hate the good in another?

The evil one watched her for many weeks despising every time she laughed. Even though when he met her, he returned a smile for a smile. Deception was who she met, but introduced as morality. She received the introduction at face value. There was no need to form an opinion at the time. So, she thought…. How often do we form an opinion too quickly? First impressions have often fooled a person. Dressed like a sheep but really a wolf.

The quote, "Don't judge a book by its cover" does not always apply. Sometime we must be in touch with the spirit, the spirit of discernment.

It seems like danger was lurking around, but she was not aware. We can all face this kind of issue as we deal with people from different walks in life.

Consider, if we lived in a shell or a closed room, the possibility of danger is less likely, but we still have to deal with our minds. A person's mind and heart can be dangerous alone. Where the heart is the mind will follow. So as a man thinks, so is he. The mind can take you places you rather not go and refuse to travel again.

Radiance met the wrong person at a bad time in his life. Maybe he was a good man in the past. Misfortune could have fallen on him and made him bitter and resentful of others. Misfortune can weigh a ton.

Let us lay aside every weight and sin, which so easily beset us, and let us run with patience the race that is set before us.

Forgiveness is light but it was apparent what he carried was heavy. Thinking of a struggle imagine, picking up a heavy object can be overwhelming. Now carry it everywhere you go. You would be easily weighed down. Have you ever heard it said "He looks like he is carrying the weight of the world on his shoulder"? That does not seem like a happy ending.

Woe to those who call evil food, and good
evil; who put darkness for light and light for
darkness; Who put bitter for sweet, and
sweet for bitter.

Isaiah 5:20

4

The meeting was casual, not knowing if their path would ever cross again.   Though it seemed impossible they were assigned to work on the same project.   She as a student doing extra work as an intern and he as a contractor.   All of Radiance's teachers loved her and thought this would give her some experience which she needed.

She had lots of good ideas and was a hard worker.   She was taught whatever you put your hands to do, do it to the glory of God.

She was always thankful for those who reached out to help her. She stayed on course to do a good job.

As full of aspiration as she was, she was no stranger to defeat. After being rejected for a job, she was depleted. She felt as if the light was out and darkness had settled on her.

Who did she meet while walking home? Who is always there when we focus on the bad and not see the goodness shining through? Where is your faith?

It was him. He smiled, a smile on his face and evil in his heart. After greetings he asked her to join him for coffee. She would have said no but her guard was down. Rejection has a way of dimming the light, so we don't see the warning signs.

While at the coffee shop she hardly said a word, which was okay because he had been talking about himself for an hour. He said a lot, she heard a little. The light had dwindled.   He realized her silence and placed his hand over her hand. The heat from his hands startled her. She thought it was from the coffee cup, but she had not noticed he finished his coffee long before her.

His actions related to compassion but his thoughts said deceit.

She was at a place where the smallest jester seems like care. When you are so far down a simple thank you can brighten your day. Now that she is listening, he turns to flattery, in which she was willing to receive. He began telling her how beautiful her eyes were. He had already sensed her weakness. He could tell by the little glow he was on the right path. She just thought she needed to feel some kind of joy whether true or false.

We should always be aware of a flattering word that are meant to entrap us. As the day grew long Radiance realize she needed to go home.   She excused herself without listening to him pleading for her to stay. She left him sitting at the coffee shop. Smart girl!   She was not ready to reveal where she lived. She did not know he already knew. The way life goes the enemy will find out your dwelling place before they receive an invitation.

The thief cometh not, but for to steal, and to
kill, and to destroy: I am come that they
might have life, and that they might have it
more abundantly.

John 10:10

5

When she was home, she felt better. She had made her home a place of peace. She invited Christ in long ago.

With the door shut and prayer open, she gave herself to Christ. She sought after redeeming grace that only Christ could give. She prayed and shed tears of joy just knowing he would help her through. She always reflected on the scripture that helps her in trials like. Proverbs 3: 5,6.

"Trust in the Lord with all thine heart; and lean not unto thine own understanding. In all thy ways acknowledge him and he shall direct thy path." Time with God always makes things better.   Understanding that God is always in control is crucial.

Even though time was tough right now, she knew that she could trust God to see her through these times of difficulty.

The phone rang to a welcome hello. It was human resources from the job she had interviewed.   The person that they chose to hire, declined the job.   This sounds like a faith test. They called her to make an offer.

She said yes! Almost too quickly!

Praises of joy filled her home. God's plan is so much better than ours.   She had a job. She was so happy.

It seemed so long ago since she was employed. The bills are many and the dollars has been few. Thanks to God, she was able to pay rent and manage as best as she could. God has always made a way.

She began to prepare for her new job. As she prepared for work, she thought about the time of being unemployed.

"Fear had captured me." I entered into a room where I lost all control. This room was called fear and I saw no exit sign. I could feel, the room consume me and the only comfort I found was in my tears. I thought it was the tears that released me but it was the prayers I prayed in the mist of my tears. There was an exit, and the only way to see it was through Jesus. Wow! How did I get in this room? I 'am ready to leave this place. I want the freedom Jesus offers me. I refuse to be bound by outside forces.

This was a trick of the enemy. It had crippled me far too long. There was no moving forward only standing still. It seemed as though I was moving but I was only going through the motions. This was not where I wanted to stay. I didn't even have to pack a bag there was nothing in this place that I wanted to carry with me.

I will hold his hand and walk out, as he leads me, this is over, and it is time to shine once again. Christ is the light of the world and I will bear witness of that light.

When the door closed behind me the enemy thought that was the end for me. What he did not know was that my God opens doors that no man can shut.

The only reason the door closed was because he does not dwell in darkness, and I was walking in darkness; however, he will light the path to the way out.

I escaped the unrighteous path of destruction. I 'am free to live, free to shine as radiant as God will allow.

There was a plan for me. Remember "For I know the plans I have for you, says the Lord. They are plans for good and not for evil, to give you a future and a hope."

 I was not aware, of the plans. Now I know, I walked away from the wrong path. Now I know, that he always knows what's best for me.

God's purpose is much higher than our plans or even our mistakes.

I will no longer focus on my past mistakes. I will walk in the radiant light of the Son.

Why do you need to know what caused me to fall into despair? Is it not enough that I have overcome?

Through Christ all things are possible. He never left me, even at the time, when I lost faith.

He knew I belonged to him.   In my weakness he is strong.

What caused my pain might be your same issue. It could be completely different but if we continue to seek Jesus, we will overcome our trials.

Forgive those that hurt you. If you refuse to forgive you allow yourself to be held in bondage. Just as God forgives us, we are to forgive one another.

If you want to walk in the light, you must step out of the darkness.

"Yea thou I walk through the valley of the shadow of death I will fear no evil for you, Lord are with me."

Know that he is God and he desires your praise and worship, first come out of the darkness. True worship is in spirit and truth.

God is love and he has given everyone a light to follow that light is Jesus. When we have made the choice to follow the light, he will direct you in the way we should go.

The path of righteousness is given in his word and once we receive the word it is written on the tablet of our heart.   The Holy

Spirit will continue to bring the word back to our remembrance daily. Make a daily choice to follow Jesus Christ. Let it shine like the light on a hill so others will see that you bear witness of the light of the world Jesus Christ!

Now the Lord is that Spirit: and where the
Spirit of the Lord is, there is liberty.

2 Corinthians 3;17

Thief

Hi, let me introduce myself.   Some call me "the thief, Lucifer, the devil, the deceiver and Satan", to name a few. Even God knows me and told you my mission, "to steal, kill and destroy." Jesus experienced me in the wilderness but he overcame my power. He told you how to discern me, for I come in many forms. I don't give up easily. I have been watching you and I find you are not a threat. You have so much unfinished business in your life, I have plenty of time to come back for you.

I'm not sure why you continue to act as if you are a Christian but I like that about you. Imagine I did not plant the seed, that was all your doing? The fact you won't forgive, works in my favor. There are so many of you that blame me for your own faults. I see you making conscious decision to remain in sin, when help is one call away.

I cased your home for many weeks after that Sunday you felt a tug, to let go and let God. You cried and felt sorrow. It stayed on your mind but you did not repent. I knew I would have lost you if you did.

You chose to hang on to the hate. You were pulled back into my trap. There might be residual affects left in your heart but right now I don't need to worry about you. You work for me. Didn't' you know if you don't work for him, you work for me? There is no in between. See you later. I need to speak with your wife I noticed she has been spending a lot of time in prayer.

Your wife received a letter from an unknown lady revealing your relationship but she did not read it. This might have concerned you but no change occurred. When you saw the letter, it should have served as a warning but you hide the letter for your protection. You failed to protect your wife and that is how I know you are mine. That was your opportunity to allow your wife to minister to you.

I see your wife kneeling to pray. She has prepared a space for prayer and meditation. This is the one place in the house you hate, as soon as she enters you find ways to interrupt, you are under my control.

My fear is that she will get a prayer through, your fear is that God will answer her prayer.

She believes you understands her prayer life as a good thing, though you understand you refuse to believe.

The faith your wife has won't allow her to be defeated. She is committed to her time to meditate on the word.

I took the time to listen as she prayed today.

 Father thank you for you are so good. You allowed your Holy Spirit to lead and guide me all through this day. You protected me from the hands of the enemy and for that I say thank you. I thank you for your love and kindness and that you continue to bless me in spite of my short comings. Please forgive me of all my sins and trespasses.

Please create in me a clean heart that I will be your worthy servant.

Please bless my church family and all the sick and those in bereavement everywhere. Comfort those who are hurting and lonely. Father God, please hear my prayer and bless me in your son Jesus's name, Amen.

I heard this prayer and was not surprised. What I dislike was the sincerity of her heart. If she keeps this up, I will have to make some drastic changes.

Some people think your wife live in a state of denial.

Sometimes she convinces me but the tears she cries let me know she is still human. So that means I have an opportunity to infiltrate her mind. A little doubt here and there planted in just the right places.

It does not matter what vehicle the doubt travel on, it just has to get to her mind. I have been known to use mom, dad, children, and friends and yes, the spouse. Actually, the list goes on and on.

The key is for her faith not to continue to grow. The reverse of it all is that the trials will cause her faith to grow if she doesn't fall first. Falling from grace is what I am seeking.

Okay, let me see how I can reach this woman. As long as she believes in the power of prayer it will be difficult. I must think a little.

I can possibly get to her through her husband, or maybe the kids. I have an even better idea. I can use the place she worships. (Judgement will start at the church). This will be a good place to start. Those people say they love each other but they are filled with envy and jealousy. They say they are filled with the Holy

Ghost. I disagree. If they were filled, it would leave no room for me. I'll just walk around seeking a way to destroy her, her faith I mean.

When a person has nothing else to hold on to, they keep their faith believing Jesus can help them through all things. Strip their faith away and they will die. The guilt and shame will lead them to the first thing that brings them pleasure and there I will be able to guide them along on their journey. This trip to hell will be exciting until the end! Did you think I wanted to be there alone?

My job is twofold I have to keep those I have and get those who are seeking Christ. Let's see what my people think of this family. I actually have someone in the neighborhood.

These nice young men desire to do my bidding. They have decided to commit a robbery. They have watched this family for weeks seeking how to carry out their plans to rob this home of their valuables.

It does not matter to me what they take, it is their actions that please me.

Some Christians are the best people to watch. Even in doing well, they are helping my cause especially on Sunday.

They leave home on Sunday morning to arrive at church. Not sure why they go to Sunday school. It's obvious they are not learning anything. They go to keep the pastor from preaching a sermon about them. Plus, it looks good since the father is a deacon.

The only thing I don't like about this is my people have to go in the church to get the full picture, this is a risk.

The people seem to love the singing but not the word so much. The word seems to put most of them to sleep. The preacher knows this, so he yells at them.   This is effective in keeping them awake but slows down the learning because now it's a game. Who can yell the loudest the preacher or the people? I know it is the truth that counts. Maybe they won't figure this out. After church they go back to their old routine.

They argue all the way home, so by the time they get home, the unity is broken. They all go to separate rooms till dinner. I have concluded that we can't do this on Sunday.

I didn't think Sunday was good anyway.

Most people do better on Sunday than any

other day of the week, so they stay home,

and they call it family time. On Monday

they hit the ground running. After Sunday

you would think, they would stop to pray.

No chance of that happening! Facebook

takes priority.   They have to check to see

what everyone else did for the weekend.

Mistake number one I know that they need

to take a good look at themselves first. We

have been watching them long enough to

know that they have their own issues to look

after. On Monday they all leave home about

the same time but come home at different

times. If Dad the deacon meets his girlfriend, he will come home and leave again to throw his wife off. He does not know she already knows. She just chooses to believe everything will get better. The son comes home after practice, he is into sports. The daughter gets lost on face book, she not really there. Mom just checks out because it is better than being there.

My people see this as a messed-up home. What do they have of value? We know they have two computers. It would do them good if we take those. The wife has plenty of jewelry. She gets something every time her husband feels guilty. There is a TV the son has. He is consumed in sports, that is his way of escape. Funny thing he does not have a Bible.

So here is the list, computers, jewelry and TV's not sure if it's worth the risk. Like I said, I don't care what they take, it is the act that matters to me. The word says what you do for Christ last, that goes double for me. The more sin you commit the less I have to worry about you.

There could be something of value in this home but sin keeps it out. Maybe there will be a hint of love, joy or peace.

You must be crazy. This home is a mess!

Why would any of those things be there?

Walk with me. They go to church surely;

they have heard something. Every Sunday,

the preacher gives them a word. At what

point do they receive it? I don't understand

why people go to church if they choose not

to follow the word. They are familiar with

the word but don't choose to follow. Could

it be for appearance? It looks good if

people go to church.

"They are good people"

Well, we know going to church does not

make you a good person.

Church can be a mask. It gives people a look or status so they can hide what they really are. Have you seen the criminals in church? Now we know all people are not like this. But at what point does a person change and follow the word? Good Question.

  Okay, okay! What are we doing here? I knew this was a risk! This seed has been planted. See what grows.

It is sad for me but it is true, Revelation gives the ending. God wins.............

Precious Stones

I wear a bracelet of precious stones every day, it was a gift from my father. The stones glisten in the sun light. Each stone was cut in a different shape, it was the most beautiful piece of jewelry I owned. I love that it's so versatile, I can wear it with most of my outfits. Shades of pink, blue, green, purple and red ascents perfectly. It was a graduation gift given before my father was deployed to war. I was sort of happy he was leaving but sad he was going to war. He seems like he was having a bad day every day.   Maybe he was holding on to frustrations.   The bracelet reminds me of happy times when family secrets were hidden people once carried their secrets to the grave and harbored resentment all their days. There was a time when it seems like love was flourishing.   It amazes me how happiness can turn into bitterness so quickly. Time did not heal the wounds. Band aids over time cause an infection that resulted in gangrene. Gangrene is when body tissue is killed due to lack of blood flow, like dreams transformed to nightmares. Sometime arms, fingers, toes or legs has to be amputated to stop the spread of the infection.   An infection can cause death and in a family this sorrow is hard to convalesce. One day I notice the bracelet in the bottom of my jewelry box. It had lost it shine but so had I. I thought I had move past the pain until today. I couldn't figure out what my dad would be so hostile towards me at times. I began to cry; I remembered what I had lost. I wanted my family back; I want to laugh and have joy. Things of monetary value replaced genuine love for people. My heart seems to split, I longed for love but found comfort in things that was constant. Mother and Father has passed on but the secrets remain. I realize the heart needs to be healed. I have let too many years separate me from reality.

I placed myself in solitude in my bed room. The room was elegant, everything was in its proper place.   The color scheme was pleasing to the palate of the eye.   All things place with appreciation of detail. The aroma filled every significant space leaving nothing lacking. This was a room designed for a queen every precious thing I desired was at my finger tip. Yet my heart desire was far from me, I sat in the most beautiful chaise lounge chair made from the finest material.   I was adorned in the most beautiful silk money could buy. Yet money could not dry my tears, I was perfect on the outside but empty on the inside. Life had afforded me with precious items to look upon but what to pay for love was out of reach.   I reached for love but riches crowded my desires. When love came near, I assume it was for sale. I lost my understanding of the cost of love; I did not grasp the idea it was not a material possession. The freedom of love is priceless like the smell of a new born baby. Love encompasses actions and emotions that dwell deeper than the surface of mere things.

Happiness for a moment can never equal joy.

In my hand I hold the bracelet of precious stones, long forgotten, each precious stone holds a million memories good and bad. Some would say stones don't hold memories but they remind me of life long ago. The life they represent holds intimate valuable treasures locked away. As I sit here today with illusions of yesterday, I feel a bit suicidal but the therapist believes it's helpful to remember. She seems to think if I talk about it, I will learn to cope with life better.

I realize that the past should not control my future but first I have to get over the past.

I hope she realize this could take a while but she gets paid by the hour. The journey from happiness to bitterness seem to happen like overnight. I woke up and there I was. The path to get past bitterness seems to be a life time. The triggers pop up too often, in smells, sounds, movies, songs the list is almost endless. I will be laughing one minute and crying the next. Then I will spend the next two days in bed re-living the past. The tears won't stop so I stay in bed till I can't cry anymore. Crying does not help anything at least that's one of the things

my dad would say.

On my twelfth birthday my parents surprised

me with a puppy, he was so cute we played

together and he listened to every word I

spoke. He was my best friend. His name

was Longfellow. Like the poet in the 1800,

dad would read some of his poem to me.

Dad often recited quotes from his work like

"Angels of life and death alike are his;

without his leave pass no threshold". As a

child I could not understand but as I grew

older and faced loss, I began to know

exactly the meaning to these words. My dad

was a strong man with strong beliefs, so I thought. He was stern, once he made up his mind on a thing, that's the way it was going to be. His unrelenting nature gain him much respect from his peers and in business. The mention of his name made people listen. I just thought my dad was important, that made me feel safe.   My family spent our vacation in Florida one year, we entered a fishing tournament. It was so much fun, dad said we were going to win and we did.   I found out later that my dad paid the judges for that win.   I now think he paid for a lot of things that I was not aware. He was my dad and I loved him.

I remember my mom as she was always full

of joy. She spent a lot of time baking

deserts just to give them all away. I think

this was her coping mechanism when the

world was not kind to her, she would be

kind to others. She always thought people

were whispering about her. Even so,

everyone looked forward to her delicious

goodies. She would bring me with her to

deliver the goodies. Sometimes, while she

was in the house, I would help myself to one

or two of the cookies. She would return to

the car smiling and singing a song. This

made her so happy I would give anything to

feel that right now.

Today is a big day, we are having guest. It's exciting because we rarely have visitors in the home. People usually speed by or slow down to view the property and keep going. Sometime the mail courier comes to the door to deliver packages but that's the sum of our activity.   Some of my parents' friends are spending the weekend. I vaguely remember them but I found some old cards and letters with their names, the Frazier's . They just wanted to spend some time on the property for old times' sake. I agreed, it would be good to hear footsteps other than mine or the servants.

The home was spotless and the smell of

eucalyptus and jasmine fill the rooms.

Even though the scent of jasmine is robust

the eucalyptus sneaks in just a bit.   My

mom loved the fragrance of the eucalyptus,

she would say I smell the healing.   I really

want the Frazier's to enjoy their time here.

Maybe I should open a bed and breakfast.

No. the staff would hate that idea, they've

gotten accustom to it being just me.   They

have been so kind to me, they have been

with me for so long, they know what to

bring me before I make a request.   I must be

a creature of habit.   Although the news of

visitors was a shock, it did not take long before they were excited as well.

My heart leaped when the guess was announced. I smiled nervously as I greeted them, they were much older than I imagine. I took pleasure in showing them around before leaving them in room to rest a while. They seem quite happy to be here as I was happy to see them.   By far this is the most exhausting day I have had in a while. I'm going to rest while they rest and get up again for dinner.

I was awakened by a loud crash. I jumped out of the bed and ran to the window. A car had crashed into the large oak tree by the road, why today! we have guest. As I made my way to the front yard the Frazier's was already present on site. It seems that someone lost control of their car while looking at the property. The guest just happencd to be taking a walk around. They witness the whole event. The young man was not injured but embarrassed about what happened, he apologized relentlessly. After the police left, we all retired inside to include the young man. He was very interested in the house and he seemed to know the other guest. It was odd they seem like friends instead of strangers. After dinner we walked to the pond and the guest reminisced about picnics by the pond with my parents.   They spoke of the fish they caught. They remembered me running around trying to catch the butterflies. This was a nice time until the young man revealed he was a private detective.   It seemed I was the only one shocked about his identity. The accident was staged to get access to the home and me. He said he was hired to find me.   I was not sure why he needed to find me, yes, I was loss but only from myself. I had no idea why anyone would be looking for me. I was intrigued by all these happenings so I entertained his story and the guest remained silent.

The young man was hired to find me because my real parents was searching for me. Something is wrong with this story, I was raised by my real parents and now they have passed, what is the meaning of this? Actually, your guest are your real parents, the Frazier's. I refuse to listen to this foolishness anymore. I ran to my room where I called the family attorney. He suggested that I calm down, he would come to the house right away. The staff was trying to figure out what was happening but

I felt like they were fully aware. Is this why they protected me all these years? When Mr. Birch the attorney arrived, I asked him to my room, I never did this before. I wanted to make sure no one was listening.

Mr. Birch revealed that the guest was my family the lady was my mother's younger sister. She was pregnant at a young age she was very upset and didn't want anyone to know. Your mother was not able to have children so they took a trip to Europe for a year. Your mother came back with a beautiful little girl. Your real mother made a promise never to interfere with you.   She promises she would tell no one of this.   She kept that promise well but I always felt that my dad was not my real dad.   Now I see that neither of them was my parents. My mom never spoke of having a sister.   It always felt like my mom was my real mother, I always felt a deep love from her. I can't believe they would let me feel like I didn't belong, why not tell me the truth?   I have been going to therapy for so many years for problems that could be fixed with a conversation.

I understand they loved me but why not tell

me the truth?   Mom never mentioned she

had a sister and my real mom was satisfied

being a friend of the family.   That all seem

unreal, why hide the truth.   They were

going to tell you but when your dad was

killed in Iraq your mother didn't want to

face it alone.   Your dad wanted to tell you

before he left but everything happened so

fast.   If you look at the bracelet he gave

you, you will see how much he loved you.

Each stone represents what he could not say.

He wanted a son for many years but your

mom was unable to have a child. This put a

strain on both of them.   He struggled to

accept you for many years but he grew to love you even though he was not sure how to express his feelings. He thought money would make up the difference. You may think the bracelet is very valuable, which it is, in love but not in price. The stones in the bracelet he found when he walked with you, he had them shaped and designed for you. When you were happy, sad, excited, disappointed or confused he place a stone for who you were. He wanted to help you through all those times.   I now feel a relief, I feel a sense of belonging but my dad is not here so I'm a little sad. It makes me sick knowing I wanted him to leave. I cleaned up the bracelet and put it on my wrist, I can

wear it again.   The love that I thought I lost

was just hidden behind secrets.   They are

now all revealed, I can remember my

parents with love and joy and I can receive

my new parent in peace.   In the end love

conquers all.